30199
L

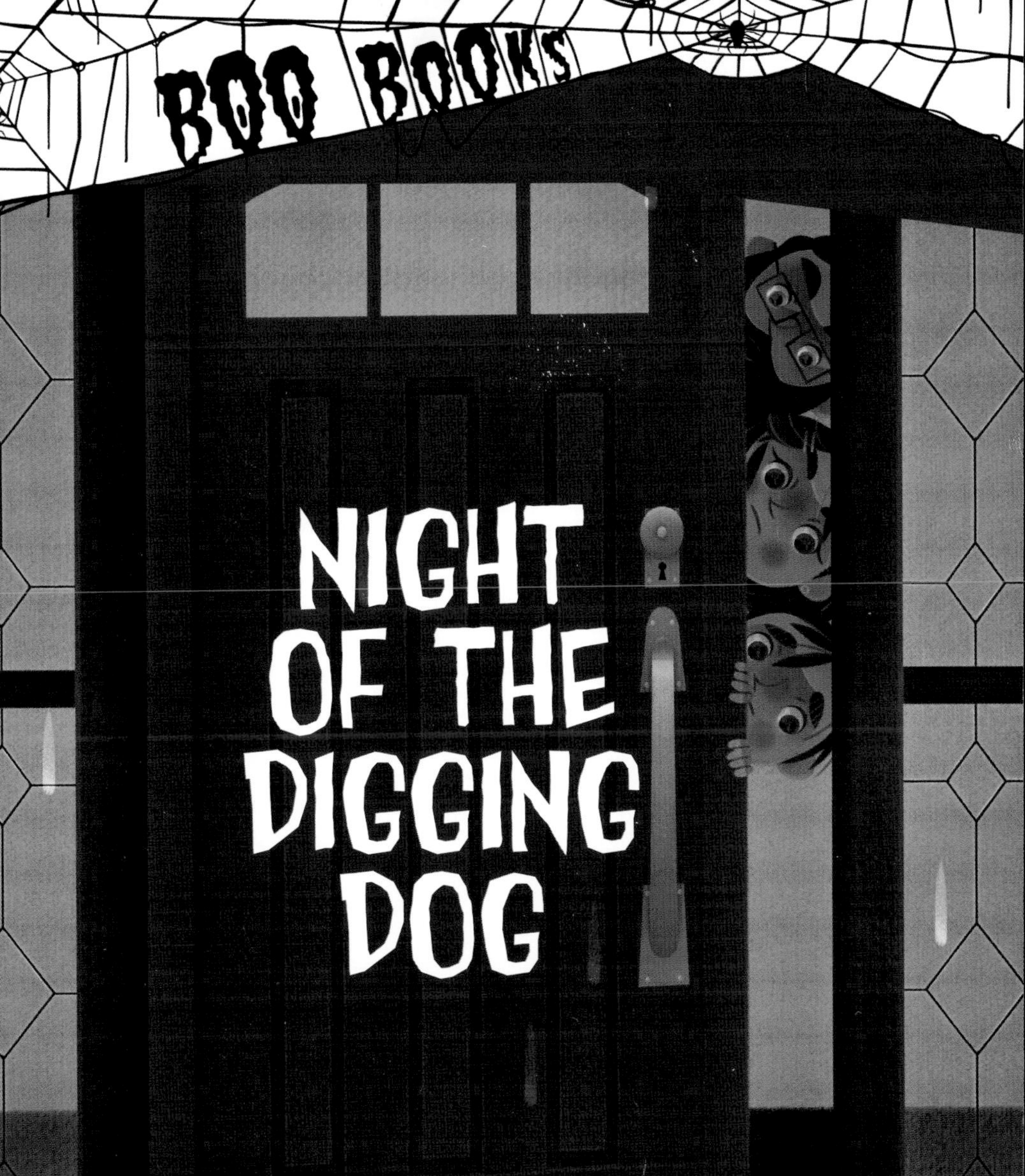

BOO BOOKS

NIGHT OF THE DIGGING DOG

by John Sazaklis

illustrated by Giada Gatti

PICTURE WINDOW BOOKS
a capstone imprint

Boo Books is published by
Picture Window Books
A Capstone Imprint
1710 Roe Crest Drive
North Mankato, Minnesota 56003
www.capstonepub.com

Library of Congress Cataloging-in-Publication Data
Sazaklis, John, author.
Title: Night of the digging dog / by John Sazaklis.
Description: North Mankato, Minnesota : Picture Window Books, [2019] |
        Series: Boo books | Summary: George's new dog is obsessed with
        the cemetery, but one night on their walk he digs up an arm
        bone—and the previous owner follows George home.
Identifiers: LCCN 2019003601| ISBN 9781515844846 (hardcover) |
        ISBN 9781515844907 (eBook)
Subjects: LCSH: Dogs—Juvenile fiction. | Cemeteries—Juvenile fiction.
        Skeleton—Juvenile fiction. | Horror tales. | CYAC: Horror stories.
        | Dogs—Fiction. | Cemeteries—Fiction. | Skeleton—Fiction. |
        LCGFT: Horror fiction.
Classification: LCC PZ7.S27587 Ni 2019 | DDC 813.6 [E]—dc23
LC record available at https://lccn.loc.gov/2019003601

Shutterstock: ALEXEY GRIGOREV, design element, vavectors, design
element, Zaie, design element

Designer: Tim Palin and Ashlee Suker
Production Specialist: Laura Manthe

Printed in the United States of America.
PA71

TABLE OF CONTENTS

CHAPTER ONE
DIG, DOG, DIG

George had always wanted a dog.

Then one day, his parents got him Romero.

Romero looked like a normal dog and did normal dog stuff.

Except for one thing.

On every walk, Romero pulled
George into the cemetery.

The dog raced through the iron
gates. He sniffed each grave in
search of something.

"This place gives me the creeps,"
George said.

One stormy night was extra creepy. Winds howled. Heavy rain made the dirt muddy and soft.

Romero stopped at an old tombstone. He sniffed the grave. Then he began to dig.

George was cold and scared.

He tugged on the dog's leash, but

Romero kept digging.

BOOM! Thunder rumbled.

Finally, Romero pulled out

something from the deep, dark

hole.

"Ahh!" George screamed.

CHAPTER TWO

FINDERS CREEPERS

Lightning flashed.

The dirt moved beneath George's feet. He looked down and saw something moving in the hole.

BOOM! Thunder crashed again.

George dropped the leash and ran for home!

George raced into his house and slammed the door.

He was dripping wet and out of breath. His heart felt like it could beat out of his chest!

Moments later, Romero ran to the backyard with his new toy.

George's parents saw the dog running around on the muddy grass.

He was acting stranger than normal.

"What is going on?" asked George's mom.

"You look like you've seen a ghost!" added his dad.

"I think I did!" said George.

"Romero found a bone in the cemetery," George began.

Suddenly, there was a knock at the door.

KNOCK KNOCK

George nearly jumped out of his boots.

"I think its owner followed us home!" George screamed.

"Don't be silly," said his dad as he opened the door.

No one was there.

CHAPTER THREE

REST IN PEACE

The rain stopped.

George's mom grabbed a
flashlight and went outside.

George and his dad followed
closely behind.

Romero was barking loudly. The family ran to the backyard.

Next to the dog stood a shadowy figure.

Mom pointed the flashlight at the figure. The light passed through most of it!

George gasped. "It's a skeleton!"

The skeleton had only one arm.

The other was in Romero's

mouth.

George's mom and dad stared in shock.

George smiled and said, "Is this your past owner?"

Romero barked and wagged his tail.

The skeleton picked up its arm
and threw it in the air.

Romero jumped and caught the
bone in his mouth.

CHOMP

George could not believe his eyes.

"They are playing catch!" he cried.

The skeleton nodded and popped its arm back in place.

Then it waved goodbye.

Romero started to dig again.

He quickly dug a big hole in the backyard. Then the dog barked at his bony friend.

"He wants to bury the skeleton in the backyard!" George said.

"Mom, Dad, can we keep it?"
George asked.

George's parents could only nod.

The skeleton gave them both a
big hug.

Then the skeleton climbed into
the freshly dug grave.

AUTHOR

John Sazaklis is a *New York Times* bestselling author with almost 100 children's books under his utility belt! He has also illustrated Spider-Man books, created toys for *MAD* magazine, and written for the BEN 10 animated series. John lives in New York City with his superpowered wife and daughter.

ILLUSTRATOR

Giada Gatti fell in love with art when she was a child, although the most artistic thing she could produce was a massive handprinted mess on the wall of her granny's hat shop. She studied web and graphic design and communication at the Santa Giulia Academy of Fine Arts in Brescia, Italy, where she first approached digital illustration. Giada is from a teeny-tiny city lost in the fog in Northern Italy.

cemetery (SEM-uh-tehr-ee)—a place where dead people are buried

grave (GRAYV)—a hole dug to bury a body in

iron (EYE-urn)—a type of heavy, silver-colored metal

normal (NOR-muhl)—regular or usual

skeleton (SKEL-eh-tuhn)—the bones that support the muscles and organs of a human

tombstone (TOOM-stohn)—a statue or other marker of where someone is buried

DISCUSSION QUESTIONS

1. Do you think the skeleton was good or bad? Explain.

2. Do you think Romero will continue to dig in the graveyard? Why or why not?

3. What is your favorite illustration in this book? Explain why.

WRITING PROMPTS

1. Writing scary stories can be a lot of fun! Try writing your own scary story to share.

2. Draw a monster. Then give the monster a name and write a few sentences about it.

3. Write a story about your own pet. If you don't have one, write about a pet that you would like to own.

SCARED SILLY JOKES!

What was the skeleton's favorite musical instrument?
The trom-bone!

How do you make a skeleton laugh?
Tickle his funny bone.

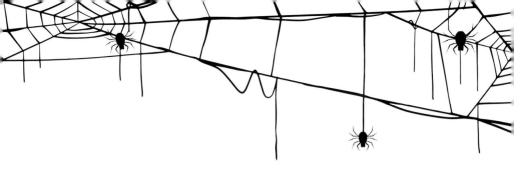

Why did the skeleton cross the road?
To get to the body shop.

What do you call a skeleton who won't finish his homework?
Lazy bones!

Who is the most famous skeleton detective?
Sherlock Bones.

How did the skeleton know it was going to rain?
She could feel it in her bones.

BOO BOOKS

Discover more just-right frights!

ATTACK OF THE CUTE

CAMPFIRE VAMPIRE

THE HAUNTED BACKPACK

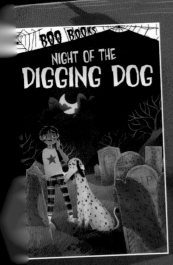

NIGHT OF THE DIGGING DOG

SCARE BALL

WITCH'S STEW

Only from Capstone